D1572768

Allie the Active Alligator

Book A of The Character Kingdom Series

Written by: Baylee Chaffin

Illustrated by: Mohamed Daamouche

Copyright © 2020 Baylee Chaffin

All rights reserved. This book or any portion thereof
may not be reproduced or used in any manner whatsoever
without the express written permission of the publisher
except for the use of brief quotations in a book review.

ISBN:979-8-6910-2935-6

For more information:
Email-bayleechaffin@thecharacterkingdom.com

Dedicated to Jackie Chaffin

Today in Character Kingdom, Allie Alligator leaves for her first day of school.

On her way to school, Allie remembers that after lunch she has gym class. She begins to get nervous because she doesn't know what sport her class will be playing today.

Allie grew up playing tag and jump rope with her siblings but has never played a sport before.

At school, Allie Alligator tries to make friends and focus on her work, so her nerves don't ruin her day.

When it's time for gym class, everyone starts to play except for Allie Alligator.

Mr. Alligator sees Allie on the bleachers and asks her why she isn't playing with her classmates.

Allie tells Mr. Alligator that she doesn't think she will enjoy playing basketball with the class because she has never played before.

After listening to Allie, he blows his whistle to gather everyone for a class meeting on the bleachers.

Mr. Alligator tells the class to always try new things. Playing basketball might be scary at first, but you'll never know how much fun you could have.

After hearing Mr. Alligator, Allie Alligator stands up to hug and thank him. She now knows that it's fun to try new things rather than to be afraid.

For the rest of class, everyone is active including Allie! She enjoys playing basketball and is glad she gave it a try.

Made in the USA
Monee, IL
22 December 2020

55360825R00017